WE ARE A DREAMTEAM

INFLUENTIAL AND EXCITING STORIES FOR CHILDREN ABOUT COURAGE, TEAM SPIRIT AND DETERMINATION

ANNABEL E. LEWIS

ISBN – 9798719325965

THIS BOOK BELONGS TO

_____

TABLE OF CONTENTS

FOREWORD

We hope you love this book and all of the stories within it. We hope that these words transport you on different adventures across the seas, over the waves and in the deep blue. From a crashing pirate ship to a seagull learning to live, you will discover the different worlds that make up the view beyond the window.

These stories will help you see the world in a new way. They will help to realise that no view is ever boring. No Sunday is ever the same. These stories will help you to see that with a little bit of imagination, the world is at your fingertips and the stories that wait for you will light up your world.

Each story in this book is completely original and has been dreamt up by the author. Accompanied by stunning illustrations, you will be thrown right into the adventure in no time. Now, snuggle up and get ready to discover the powers of imagination.

1. RU AND GRANDMA SEE THE WORLD

It's a Sunday like any Sunday. Gusts of wind make the ocean waves crash against the rocks. Steam rises from the pans on the stove. Mum is cooking broccoli and green beans to have with the roast chicken. The kettle boils for the gravy. The radio hums by the toaster. In the living room, the TV roars in the corner, Dad is watching a film. Raindrops trickle down the windows of the Lighthouse. It's not really a lighthouse, that's just what Grandma calls it because it was built right next to the beach and because of the big flashing light all the way at the top of the building. She says the light helps the stars to know where to gather at night. Ru lives on the 11th floor with Mum, Dad and Grandma. Not too high, but just high enough to see the ocean and the beach below. Ru and Grandma sit in the living room, watching the waves and the rain drops and Benny, the black cat, as he rolls around on the carpet.

"Sundays are boring," says Ru.

"Well, today was never going to be any more fun than last Sunday, your birthday," Grandma says, chewing on a toffee.

"I wish every Sunday was my birthday."

"Then you would be over 400 years old. Like me," Grandma says. Ru laughs, thinking about the wrinkles someone who is 400 would have. There's no way Grandma is 400 years old.

"How can you be bored when you're looking out of the window?" Grandma asks.

"It's boring outside too," Ru replies.

"Oh, come on now. It might not be very lively in here, but outside there is a whole world of excitement," says Grandma. Ru huffs and snuggles closer to Benny.

"Why don't we go up to the top floor and see what we can see from up there?" Grandma asks.

"No! I'm never going up there!"

Ru has always been scared of the top floor. It is the highest part of the building: 100 floors up, way above the clouds. Grandma says that if you hold your cheek to the window at night on the 100th floor, you can feel the heat from the stars. She also says that if you stand completely still, you can feel the building swaying in the wind. But Mum says that's rubbish.

You see, Ru doesn't ever want to go to the 100th floor because Ru doesn't like heights. Dad took Ru up to the top floor when they first moved in, but Ru's legs started to feel funny and Ru had to walk back down the stairs like a jellyfish.

"I'm never going up there!" shouts Ru.

"Oh, Ru," says Grandma. "From up there, you can see the whole world." Ru looks at Grandma. There's no way you can see the whole world, Ru thinks.

But… what if you can.

"No you can't," Ru says.

"How do you know?" Grandma replies.

What if you can see the whole world, Ru thinks.

"The whole world?" Ru asks.

"The whole world," Grandma promises.

"We can take it one step at a time," says Grandma. Ru looks up the stairs. They spiral and spiral and twist and turn and twist some more. All the way to the top. Ru puts one foot on the first step. And then another. Then another. Ru and Grandma climb step by step, calmly and slowly.

Benny must have escaped! He dashes past Grandma and Ru, 3 steps at a time! Running and climbing like a mountain lion.

"Benny!" Ru shouts, and starts running up the stairs after him.

"Ru!" Grandma shouts, and starts chasing after Ru.

Ru and Grandma run up the stairs as fast as they can, floor by floor. Without them realising, they run up high into the clouds, through the rain, and into the blue Sunday sky. Airplanes fly past them. Birds in formation swoop through the air just outside. Lightning flickers in a storm cloud only a few hundred feet away. As they climb higher and higher, the staircase becomes narrower and narrower. Not many people go up to the top floor, which is why it is old and rickety. Each step creaks and dust sheds into Grandma's hair. Scared spiders dart into dark corners when Ru runs through. Grandma does not notice the cobwebs and they get tangled in her hair. By the time she reaches the top, it looks like she is wearing a shower cap made out of spiders and silk!

"Benny! Benny!" Ru shouts. At the top of the stairs is a hatch. It's the only way to the 100th floor. Benny jumps up on the final step and rubs his face onto the corner, purring loudly. Ru collapses onto the step next to him, tired and out of breath.

"Grandma! Grandma!" Ru shouts. Grandma huffs and puffs up the steps, pushing on her knees for support and clinging tightly onto the bannister. A spider dangles off of her ear.

"I thought we… I thought… I thought we were going to take it one step at a time?" Grandma says as she tries to get her breath back. "At least, at this rate, we'll be back in time for tea."

Ru pushes the hatch open and Benny jumps through into the bright room. Ru climbs in after and then Grandma follows. Windows stretch all around. It is so much more beautiful than Ru remembers. The clouds float below like snow on the ground. Birds jump and dive through the air like fish in the sea. A small man with a big moustache peers through the window as he guides his hot air balloon past the building. But then Ru's legs start to feel like jelly. They start to feel like squiggly lines on a page and Ru falls, hugging the floor with open arms.

"I want to go back down," Ru says into the floorboards.

"Oh, come on now, Ru. Look how far you've come already. It was only 10 minutes ago that you didn't want to come up here at all! Now look at you." Ru looks up at Grandma, takes in a deep breath and then starts to crawl closer and closer to the windows. Grandma walks right up to the glass with Benny in her arms. "Look Ru," she says. "You can see the world."

"That's not the whole world!" Ru shouts. "That's just the ocean! We can see that from the sofa!"

Grandma laughs. "Look closer, Ru. What do you see?"

Ru focuses on the sea, looking up and down for anything interesting. "I see… I can see a boat! It looks like a pirate ship from up here!" Ru looks at the rocks by the beach. "I can see… I see people! They look like fish jumping in and out of the water like that!" Ru says.

"And what do you see in the sky?" Grandma asks.

"I see… I see an airplane. With smoke coming out of it!"

Grandma smiles and places her hand on Ru's head. "Up here, Ru, nothing is boring."

2. THE STOWAWAYS

Agatha and her two brothers, Martin and Arthur, had been hiding in the storage cabin of the ship for six hours since they left the port. Martin stole a necklace from the richest woman in the city, so they had to escape by boat, otherwise the police would catch them and they would be thrown in the dungeons. They did not want that to happen. So, they climbed on board the first ship they could see. Little did they know it was a pirate ship.

"I can't see anything!"

"Shhh!"

"What?"

"Be quiet!"

"What did she say?"

"Shhhh!"

The hatch opens and the bright Sunday afternoon beams into the cabin. The smell of fish and the sound of seagulls floods down into darkness. Thud. Thud. Thud. Each step echoes through the ship. Thud. Thud. Thud.

"I thought I errd somethin' down eeer!" says a pirate with a scraggly beard, blackened teeth and fingernails as long as his fingers. He walks deeper into the cabin. Lanterns swing from side to side as the waves hit against the ship. Rats scuttle along the wooden beams and water drips, drips, drips. The pirate's big gold tooth sparkles in the sun as he searches for the voices.

"Best not be any stowaways down eeer," the pirate says as he searches every corner, lifting up old, dirty blankets and peering into boxes. "You know what we do with stowaways?" he asks, softly. "We make them walk the plank," he whispers.

GULP.

"That's strange for a barrel to make a noise like that," the pirate says as he steps, thud, thud, thud, towards the barrels. The smell of rum and wine wafts around as he moves. He pulls out his sword, ready to deal with whatever is lurking in the supplies. "You best hope I don't catch you…"

Just as the pirate is about to lift the lid on the barrel, his fingers tightly gripped around the wood, the ship's commander, the famous Captain Black Eye, shouts from the deck: "I need everyone up eer, now! All hands on deck!" The pirate turns around as fast as he can and runs out of the darkness and back up the steps, slamming the hatch shut. There is silence as the slam rings out around the cabin. The only noise is the water outside and a rat nibbling on an old carrot.

"Phew! That was close," says Martin, climbing out of the barrel and brushing cabbage off of his clothes.

"If it wasn't for me, he would have caught us," says Agatha, lifting her head out of her barrel and sending a few onions rolling across the floor. "That was too close. We have to be more careful." The two children stand still, waiting for the lid to pop off of the third barrel and for their brother to climb out. "Arthur?" Agatha asks. "Are you alright?" They hear a gurgle, and then another and another. All of a sudden, the lid bursts off of the barrel and Arthur comes shooting out, spraying Martin and Agatha in the liquid he was submerged in. Arthur gasps for air.

"Gross!" Agatha shouts.

"What is that?" says Martin.

"Vinegar… I think!" Arthur says, shaking his hair like a dog and spraying more liquid all over the place.

"You were holding your breath for all that time?" Agatha asks.

"It stinks," says Martin. Arthur licks his fingers and smiles at his siblings. "What do we do now?"

"We just have to keep quiet and hope they don't come back down here," says Agatha.

"I can't get back in there," Arthur says.

"Well, I'm not swapping," says Martin.

"It's your fault we're on this ship anyway! If you hadn't stolen that necklace, we wouldn't have had to escape!" Arthur exclaims.

"Well, you're still not getting in my cabbage! I'm the eldest and what I say goes," Martin says.

"We're triplets! You're only older by 3 minutes!" Arthur shouts, even louder.

"Boys!" Agatha interrupts. "If we stay quiet, none of us will have to get in the vinegar. Now shush!" The two boys glare at each other. Vinegar drips off of Arthur's nose and a piece of cabbage is lodged in Martin's hair, but Arthur doesn't tell him. He thinks it looks quite funny.

Martin climbs up onto one of the beams, pushing a sleeping rat off. He positions himself with his legs hanging over the edge. Then, he grips his legs around the wood and lets his whole body drop down, so he's hanging upside down like a bat. The stolen necklace starts to slip out of his pocket but he catches it before it hits the ground. The jewels dazzle his eyes. They reflect light all around the cabin and onto the ceiling like stars at night.

"As long as we have this," Martin starts. "We will be rich everywhere we go." Martin leans closer to kiss the necklace right on its biggest diamond but a rat the size of a small dog likes the look of those sparkling jewels and jumps off of the beam and grabs it with its dagger-like teeth. "Hey!" Martin shouts. The rat lands on the floor, necklace in its mouth, and watches the children as they stare at the rat carrying their fortune.

"Get it!" Agatha screams.

They all charge after the rat which is heading for the stairs. They try and jump on it but the rat slips through their grasp. The three of them burst through the hatch onto the top deck, right in front of the deadly pirates.

The pirates grab the siblings, throwing them over their shoulders and marching them to the plank. The pirates cheer and watch as the children are lined up, ready to be thrown off into the choppy waters. Agatha closes her eyes and thinks of home. Arthur's teeth chatter together with fear. Martin tries to pinch himself and wake up from this nightmare.

"Walk the plank!" a pirate shouts.

CRASH.

They think that must be the sound of the water swallowing them whole. But it is not. It is the sound of the ship crashing into the rocks. Wooden splinters fly through the air. Parrots shoot off into the sky. The pirates jump over the side as the ships in half. The plank that Agatha, Martin and Arthur are standing on snaps under their weight and they go tumbling into the sea.

The pirates stand on a big floating wooden platform with gold, wine and clothes all around them. "Listen up!" one of the pirates shouts. "The Captain seems to have drifted out to sea. Now he has gone, I will be your new leader."

"No you won't!" another shouts.

"I'm the strongest!" one says from the back.

"I should be captain because I have stolen the most gold!"

"I'm the loudest!"

"I'm the most handsome!"

"I have the longest toe nails!"

"I have the most gold teeth!"

"I'm the drunkest!" one pirate shouts as he floats by on his back.

The pirates squabble and argue and shout, soon they start to push each other and wrestle one another to the ground.

"Quick!" Agatha says. "We have to go now, whilst they are all arguing!"

The three of them start to kick and kick and try to get the plank as far away from the pirates as possible. They kick and kick some more but the plank does not seem to move!

"We are not going anywhere!" says Arthur.

"Kick harder!" Martin shouts.

"Everybody stop!" Agatha says. "We're not going anywhere because we're all trying to push the plank in different directions! We have to work together. Boys, swim over to this side. That's it. Now, kick as hard as you can!"

The plank starts to move at great speed. The waves carry them even further and before they even realise, the pirates are almost out of sight. When Agatha turns around, she can see the wooden platform and the pirates start to sink. If only they had worked together like we did, she thinks, then they might have made it to shore.

"Look!" shouts Arthur. "I can see a lighthouse in the distance! Let's keep swimming towards that!"

The four children kick and kick, working hard as a team to get back to land. Dolphins glide through the water around them. Whales blow rockets of water into the sky. An airplane glides overhead and the big rat with the necklace in its mouth sits comfortably on the corner of the plank.

3. THE FASTEST MERMAID IN THE OCEAN

Today is the day. The big day. The day everyone has been waiting for. It all comes down to this. This is what Clara, the fastest mermaid in the world, is thinking as she lines up for the World Underwater Championships. Every mermaid in the ocean has been talking about this race for weeks. Sea creatures have travelled hundreds of miles to be here. Clara looks to her left and to her right. She sees whales, dolphins, crabs, sharks, pufferfish, even sea cucumbers. They are all here to watch me win, she thinks.

"We will not let a silly shipwreck ruin our big sporting event!" says a sea cow. There was talk of calling off the race because pieces of wood were floating down from the surface, but nothing could stop the big race.

The mermaids get ready at the starting line. Clara looks over at her rivals. Her enemies. She spots one other contestant in the race… Dash. Everyone calls her Dash because of how fast she is. But Clara has beaten her in every race. But she's still the one to keep an eye on. Dash's manager, a nasty, slimy stingray, barges his way out of the spectators and calls Dash over. Clara watches, hoping her manager will say she cannot race.

"If you don't win, Dash!" the stingray yells. "If you don't win this race, I'll make sure you never race again!"

Clara watches Dash nod and swim back to her starting position. Dash tries to not make it obvious, but Clara sees her wipe away a tear.

"On your marks!" shouts the sea cow. "Get set!"

BANG.

A blue whale lets out a jet of water to signal the start of the race. And they are off! It is hard to get in front of all the racers at the start, there are too many of them. They jostle and collide and their fins bash together as they each try and get in front of the crowd. Water bubbles make it difficult to see where to go, and the first casualties of the race are thrown out of the bundle and into the spectators. The nurse sharks swim over with a stretcher and take them away.

Clara finds a gap to squeeze through and break away from the swarm of racing mermaids. She squeezes through and then launches herself away. The crowd behind her are blinded by the stir of water she leaves in her wake. She's free. Now all I have to do is focus on winning, she thinks. Clara beats her tail against the water as hard as she can, gaining more and more distance away from the other racers.

Clara glides down through the sea anemones, waving to the clown fish as she passes. Then she twists and turns through the corral, making sure she does not cut herself on the razor sharp edges. A squid must have not heard there was a race today and wakes up when Clara zooms past. He huffs and slides away underneath a rock.

After the corral, Clara speeds up towards the sunken ship. She darts in through one of the windows and into what must have been the dining hall. Gold lines the ceilings and the red carpet is still bright red. A few mussels and clams stick to the walls and seaweed sways with the current. She swims underneath a table and then through into the corridor. Chandeliers hang from the ceilings. Clara looks up at them and admires how beautiful they are. But she should not have slowed down.

Dash comes speeding up behind Clara, knocking the tables out of the way and forcing the chandeliers to swing from side to side. Clara pushes off as hard as she can but by that time Dash is right up beside her. They are tail and tail. Each one of them trying to get an inch in front. They race down the corridor and then into the engine room, squirming around the pipes and trying not to swim head first into an old coal engine. Clara spots the exit, a window at the top of the ship. She puts her head down and beats her tail, trying to get ahead. But Dash is faster than Clara remembers and it is too difficult to get away from her. They both try and get through the window but they cannot both fit through. They wedge together until they are completely stuck.

"Get away from me!" shouts Dash.

"Go back to 2nd place!" Clara replies.

They squirm and wriggle and push as hard as they can to get through until they both are set free by the sliminess of their scales. They fight to get ahead. Dash whips her tail at Clara and Clara nudges her back, trying to throw her off course.

"DEEP SEA AHEAD" reads the sign in front of them. Soon the sand and the rocks start to disappear and before either of the mermaids realise, they are at the edge of the deep sea. It is just water, as far as the eye can see. Water and darkness.

Dash screeches to a halt at the cliff edge. "I… I… I didn't know we would have to swim in the deep sea," she says, terrified. "I don't think I can do it."

"What? You scared?" Clara laughs.

"Yes, I am," replies Dash. "Ever since I was young and I got lost in the deep sea, I haven't ever been able to go back in."

Clara laughs some more and starts swimming down into the deep sea. But she hears Dash crying behind her, standing on the edge. Clara remembers Dash's manager saying that if she does not win this race, he will make sure she never races again.

Clara turns around and swims back to Dash. "Let's do it together," says Clara.

"No, it's fine. Just go," replies Dash.

"No! We will do it together." Clara sees the rest of the mermaids swimming through the exit of the ship. "We have to do it now!"

Clara grabs Dash's hand and pulls her off the edge, down into the deep sea, past the scary fish with a light bulb hanging off of its head, past the hungry sharks, and the jellyfish with tentacles miles long, past crashed submarines and over the jets of volcanic air. Clara pulls her all the way.

Soon, the finish line is in sight and the two mermaids can hear the chants. Clara stops and turns to Dash.

"You go first," she says.

"I can't do that... You helped me," Dash replies.

"There will be more races for me," Clara starts. "But if you don't win this one, there won't be any more for you. Sometimes, doing the right thing isn't about what you want, it's about helping other people get what they want."

The biggest smile covers Dash's face. "Thank you," she says.

Clara helps Dash launch off and cross the finish line. Clara comes in just behind - 2nd place, for the first time in years.

But as Clara watched Dash lift up the trophy, she knew it took courage to do something like that. Dash smiles at Clara as the ribbon is put around her neck. Dash would never forget what Clara did today.

4. THE NET

"Wow, what a race!" Olly, a small and plump octopus says as the day draws to an end. "My money was on Clara winning, though. I can't believe Dash took the trophy!"

"Yes, what a sight!" says Mark, Olly's dolphin friend. "Do you think Dash likes me?" he says.

"No way!" Olly replies. "She only looked at you because your sign says *DASH, I LOVE YOU*."

"I guess you're right."

The two friends leave the crowd and swim towards their favourite place to eat. "Can we have a table for two, please?" The waiter takes them to their table – a small rock by some seaweed. "Best seat in the house!" Olly says to the waiter.

"I think I'll have the barnacle soup."

"Me too!"

Olly looks out over the rocks and sees Dash swimming away. "Look!" Olly shouts. "That's Dash."

"Oh yes," Mark says, embarrassed.

"Want me to go get you her autograph?" Olly asks.

"No! No way. She won't want to be bothered," Mark replies.

"Oh come on!" Olly says as he gets up from his seat. "You need her autograph if you are really her biggest fan!"

"No, Olly. Come back!" Mark calls after him. But it's too late, Olly is swimming up to Dash.

Mark watches Olly approach her. She laughs and smiles. Olly holds his tentacles to try and disguise his nerves. He gets out a pen and picks up a shell from the sea bed for her to sign. Mark watches her write her name down and pass the shell to Olly. Wow, he really did it, he thinks. Dash hugs Olly and then turns and waves at Mark. He slides underneath the rock and tries to hide. How embarrassing, he thinks. Dash swims off and Olly turns to Mark, waving the shell and smiling.

"Look!" Olly shouts. "I got it!"

But what's that roar? Mark thinks. That rumble. That sound. Is it far away or close by? Mark cannot make out what it is. It sounds like an earthquake but there has not been one in years. It sounds like a hungry belly but Mark is not even that hungry. Then Mark notices the crowd left over from the race start to swim as fast as they can in the opposite direction, away from Mark and Olly. Even the waiter drops the tray and swims off. Mark looks up above him. He quickly realises what the rumbling sound is. It is no earthquake. It is no hungry belly or angry whale. That sound is the sound of a fishing boat, and the net is coming this way.

"OLLY!" Mark shouts, launching himself up and knocking over his barnacle soup. But Olly is too busy admiring the shell to notice what is happening. "OLLY!" Mark shouts again. This time Olly looks up, but it is too late. Mark watches the net fly over his head like a dark cloud. "OLLY!"

Olly does not have enough time to swim out of the way and the net scoops him up and drags across the sea bed. Mark calls out, swimming behind the net as fast as he can, but the fishing boat picks up speed and the net gets pulled further away until Olly and the net are almost completely out of sight.

Mark keeps swimming until he cannot swim anymore. "Help!" he calls out. "Help!"

"Stop your yelling!" a grumpy clam snaps.

"My friend is in that net!" Mark replies.

"Yeah?" says another dolphin. "We all have friends in those nets. That's just the way life works. Find another friend."

This makes Mark angry and he storms over to the dolphin. "No, I will not find another friend," Mark shouts. "You may just happily accept that the nets are just part of life, but I will not. I'm going to get my friend."

The dolphin looks at Mark and then at the clam. "I'll come with you," says the clam.

"Thank you," Mark replies. "But I'm not sure you will be much help. We need to stop that boat."

"Good," says the clam. "I don't really want to come. I quite like my rock."

"I'll come with you," says the dolphin.

"Thank you," says Mark.

"Wait here," the dolphin says and then swims off into the seaweed.

Mark waits and waits and starts to think the dolphin was lying and has abandoned him. He starts to worry that the boat and the net and Olly will be too far away. Just before Mark sets off alone, the dolphin returns, but not by himself.

"Is it okay if I bring some friends?" says the dolphin.

Mark watches dozens and dozens of dolphins, fish, sharks and whales come through the seaweed.

"We're here to help!" they all yell. "Let's go get our friends back!"

"Let's go!" Mark shouts and the army of sea creatures swim like fighter airplanes through the water. Soon, the net is in sight, still flying through the sea at great speed.

"There it is!" says Mark. They speed up and break into two groups. One goes left and the other goes right. And then the two groups split into four groups. Two go in front of the boat, two stay by the net. The whales grip onto the net with their small teeth. The squid places its suction cups onto the bottom of the boat and then reaches onto a rock on the ground and ties itself around it. The sharks position themself where the net meets the boat.

"On three!" Mark shouts.

"One! Two! Three!" The dolphins fly up out of the water and land onto the boat's deck. The sharks start chewing on the net. The whales start pulling the net backwards. The dolphins roll around the boat and the fishermen scream and run around, trying to get away from the dolphins. The boat starts to come to a stop and the dolphin dive back into the water. The sharks bite the net free and the whales pull the net back the way it came, with all of their friends inside. The animals swim away. The mission is a success. But the fishermen stand on the boat with their hands on their hips, angry at the sea creatures.

"Place it here!" Mark shouts.

The whales drop the net on the sea bed and it opens up, releasing all of the fish, dolphins and other animals. They swim back to their family and friends. After all of the fish have left the net, only Olly is left at the bottom of the net. Olly swims up to Mark and hugs him with all of his tentacles.

"Thank you, thank you, thank you!" Olly says. "I thought I was done for."

"Well," Mark starts. "I couldn't have done it without this team. We all worked together. It's thanks to them that we managed to set you free."

"We make a great team," says the dolphin, putting his fin around Mark.

"Oh, Mark?" Olly says.

"Yes?"

"Here," says Olly, passing him the shell signed by Dash.

5. HOW TO CATCH FISH

"Quick! Go now whilst everyone is distracted by that fishing boat!" says the mother seagull to her daughter, Sally.

"No Mum! I'm too scared!"

"Just go!"

"No!"

The two seagulls sit on the rocks watching the fish in the water below. On the beach, big red, sunburnt bodies are stacked on top of each other. Multicoloured dividers separate families. Grandmas wear big floppy hats and read books in the shade of umbrellas stuck in the sand. An ice cream van plays its tune in the car park and swarms of kids gather around it, screaming at the window.

"I want a cone!"

"Chocolate!"

"Flake!"

"Got any strawberry sauce?"

"I just want a lemonade!"

"I want 36 scoops! One chocolate chip and the rest just chocolate!"

"My mum says I can't have ice cream!"

Back on the beach, the male humans wriggle on their bellies and push themselves up with their hands, onto their knees and then onto their feet. Knocking over an almost empty can, they waddle towards the sea, belly first, and then flop into the water, sending a wave all the way into the horizon.

"Look, go now!" the mother seagull says to Sally.

"No, Mum!" Sally replies.

"Sally, the fish won't hurt you. They will never know you have dived into the water and taken one. Just go!" the mother seagull says.

You see, it is Sally's first time catching fish from the shallow waters of the beach. It's the job that every seagull has to do, but no one enjoys their first time doing it. It is far too scary, Sally thinks.

"What if… What if I dive too deep and I end up below the surface and can't get out!" Sally says to her Mum.

"Oh Sally, in all of my years of catching fish, that has only ever happened three times."

Sally gulps and stares at her Mum in shock.

"Go now!" Sally's Mum says.

"No!"

"Yes! Sally, if you don't go, we won't eat. Sometimes you have to confront your fears to get over them. After this time, you'll be able to catch fish like a natural," promises Sally's Mum.

Sally huffs and puffs. She does not want to do it. Can't someone else do it? She thinks. But she has to learn some day.

"Okay," she says.

"That's my girl. Just fly down, grab a fish or two from the water and fly back. And try not to drop them," her Mum says.

Sally beats her wings and jumps off of the rock, launching herself into the air. The target is in sight. She aims for the shallowest part of the water where the fish can be seen swimming just under the surface. All I have to do, she thinks, is swoop down, grab a fish (or two) and fly back. That's it.

Sally gets closer and closer and the smell of sun tan cream and chips dances around her beak. She swoops down, directly towards the target. Her beak approaches the water but she gets too scared! So she pulls back up into the air and flies back around for another go. She swoops down again, this time pecking her beak below the water. But her whole face is submerged. The fish scream and they all dart off in different directions.

"I can't do this! I can't. I can't. I can't!" Sally squawks.

Sally flies back to the rock where her Mum is sat and does not stop until she gets there.

"I told you I didn't want to do it!" Sally says.

"But Sally you were so close!"

"I'm not going again! I almost drowned in the water!"

"Don't be silly, Sally. I have never known one seagull to dive too deep into the water when catching fish."

"Well I could be the first!" Sally says.

"Just once more, Sally. Try one more time," her Mum says.

"No!" Sally squawks.

"Sally, you can't expect to succeed the first time you try. Sometimes you have to keep trying to get what you want," Sally's Mum says. "Do you know how many tries it took me to successfully catch fish? Thirteen. But I didn't stop trying because I knew I had to do it and I could do it. And I know you can do it. Please, Sally. Try again."

Sally glares at her Mum. "Alright," she says. "But if I don't get them this time then I'm not trying again until tomorrow."

Sally's Mum nods. "Go on then. Just remember, you can do it."

Sally sets off again, heading for the fish who have started swimming in the same spot again. She gains as much speed as possible, flies higher into the sky above the visible, fishy target and then dives down like she is an eagle hunting a mouse. Sally aims right where she went last time, forces her beak below the water and grabs two fish at once.

"Oi!" the fish shout. But that does not scare Sally this time.

She beats her wings at the fish and they dart away from her. This time, they are the scared one. Sally smiles and flies back to the rock, next to her Mum.

"Well done, Sally! I knew you could do it. And you got so many!" Sally smiles and enjoys her fish. "What did I tell you, Sally. If you try once and you don't succeed, you try again and hope you do. Even then, if you don't get the result you want, you find the determination inside of you and keep trying until you do. One day, Sally, you will be the best fish catcher in the world! … All because you keep trying and never give up."

6. WHALE ON THE ROCKS

The water hits the side of the boat with the power of an elephant ramming a safari car. The waves splash over the side and send water way up into the air, before crashing down on the crew driving the boat. But they are used to it. They know how to handle the seas. This is not just any crew. This is the crew of a lifeboat, always on the water and lending a helping hand to anyone that needs it. Today, it is not a sinking pirate ship or a fishing boat that lost a fight with some dolphins, it is a baby blue whale heading towards the rocks that needs their help. The crew on the lifeboat know they have to get there before the whale, otherwise the baby animal will be trapped in the rising tide and not be able to battle against the waves and break free. They ride across the waves. The boat jumps into the air and slams back down onto the water.

"There it is!" shouts one of the crew. "Over there! It's getting close to the rocks! We're not going to get there in time," he says.

The lifeboat is strong, it is made for the harsh waters. But it is not the fastest lifeboat that the lifeguards on this coast have. The crewmate pushes down the throttle and the boat moves faster, but not fast enough.

"It won't work! We need a faster boat!"

The crewmates grab the emergency phone from the cabinet and make a call back to base.

"Base, this is boat 004. We need some assistance. This boat isn't fast enough. By the time we get to the animal, it will be trapped in the rocks." They hang up the phone and keep driving towards the whale, trying to close in on the baby animal.

Like pans dropping on a kitchen floor or lightening striking the ground, a roar of an engine bursts across the bay. The sound of boat 001. The fastest boat the lifeguards have. It rockets towards the whale, soaring above the water. The crewmates of boat 001 have to wear goggles and strap themselves into the seats because of how fast the boat travels.

"This is 001," the radio on boat 004 blurts out. "We have the whale in sight. We reach it in around 17 seconds. Over."

The crew of boat 004 watch as 001 races towards the whale at great speed. 001 then turns and drives right in front of the whale. But the baby does not stop. 001 loops around the animal once more and drives in front of it, revving the engine and trying to scare the animal back into the deep sea. But nothing. 001 is not big enough to scare the whale off. We need a bigger boat, the crew of boat 001 think.

"This is 001. We're going to need some assistance from 009."

"009?" the voice on the other end asks.

"Yes, 009."

The two boats join together and drive next to the whale, slowly heading towards the rocks. They start to think that 009 is not coming and they will not be able to stop the whale from getting trapped. Just as they start to lose all hope, they hear the sound of 009 in the distance.

Chug, chug, chug, chug. A low hum of an engine and the whistle of steam from a chimney. 009 plods its way towards the whale. Joining the other two boats, they drive as a fleet alongside the animal.

The crew of 001 throw a rope over to 009, who ties it onto the front of the boat. 001 then pushes down the throttle and pulls 009 in front of the whale. 004 pulls up alongside the whale and uses its strength to stop the animal from going around 009. Realising the whale cannot go forward, it stops. The baby looks around for any direction to go in. But all the ways towards the rocks are blocked by the boats. The crew watch the whale as it decides what to do, hoping it will turn around. The whale dives deeper into the water and then shoots up to the surface, flipping itself over and heading back in the direction of the sea, away from the rocks.

The crew cheer and continue to follow the whale back deeper into the sea until it is far enough away from the shore that it is safe. The crew all know that they would not have been able to save the whale if it had not been for the unique skills each boat has. As a team, they were able to help the whale. But if they tried to stop it by themselves, the whale would have been trapped. Sometimes, one person's skills are not enough and team work is the best way to get the job done.

7. CRASH LANDING

"It's in sight! I can't believe it! Look, over there! We are nearly home," shouts the airplane captain. He's an old man with big bushy eyebrows and a moustache that looks like a slug on his top lip. "I can't believe it!" The old captain squints as the sun shines into his eyes, but he can still see land. The captain and his co-pilot, Lottie, have been flying around the world for the past ten years. They took off by the Lighthouse and now they will land by the Lighthouse. All they have to do is make it over the bay and onto the ground.

But flying around the world has not been an easy task. Absolutely not. You see, the captain's airplane is not like a plane you and I know. No way. It is made entirely of wood! And it does not have an engine. All it has to keep it going are peddles. The captain and Lottie have peddled the airplane around the world like they would peddle a bike. Their legs have been aching for ten years, but now they are the most muscly legs anyone has ever seen!

"Not far now, Lottie! Not far at all!" the captain says.

"Thank goodness! My legs could do with a rest! We haven't stopped since Denmark."

"Well, we can have a big rest when we touch down. I'm sure there will be a big crowd waiting for us," says the captain.

"Oh, yes!" Lottie says. "I'm sure lots of people will be waiting for us! We've become quite famous since we first took off."

"Only a few miles to go!" shouts the captain.

They peddle and peddle, knowing soon they will be able to rest their legs in a nice hot bath. Lottie pictures it in her mind. She imagines the sleep she will have as if it were the most realistic dream. It has been years since she slept in her own bed. She could sleep forever. But little does Lottie know, her bed is further away than she realises.

BANG.

"What was that?" Lottie shouts.

The captain turns around in his seat to try and see what that noise was. "Oh gosh," he says. "No no no! This can't be happening!" The captain starts to see what the noise was. The left wing is starting to snap off. "Must've hit something. Or could've been a lost bit of lightening." The captain scratches his head and strokes his moustache. "Keep peddling!" he shouts to Lottie. "I'm going to try and fix it!"

The captain gets up out of his seat and straight away Lottie has to peddle twice as hard to make up for the fact the captain is not helping. Her legs start hurting more than ever but she is distracted from the pain by the beautiful sunset and the outline of the Lighthouse in the distance.

The captain balances on the wooden frame of the plane and shuffles along the side towards the wing. He has to remind himself not to look down, otherwise the drop all of the way down to the sea is enough to make you lose your balance. Then he would fall down into the depths of the sea. Who knows what sorts of sea creatures and killer sharks live down there. The captain closes his eyes and takes in a deep breath. He has climbed along the side of the plane whilst high in the sky many times, but he has never had to fix a broken wing.

Lottie tries to turn around in her seat and make sure the captain has not fallen off but it is difficult to focus on peddling at the same time. "Captain? Captain!" she calls out. But nothing. Just the sound of the plane travelling through the sky and the birds flying below. The sound of seagulls. "Captain?"

"I don't think I can fix it!" the captain shouts back. "We have to try and land as soon as possible." He shuffles along the plane back into his seat and starts peddling again.

"C'mon, we need to peddle harder!" the captain shouts. The plane is still a couple of miles off shore. They still have a lot of peddling to do.

BANG.

CRUNCH.

SNAP.

"That doesn't sound good!" says Lottie as the plane starts to tilt to the left and begin falling down towards the sea.

"And that doesn't feel good!" says the captain.

"We're going to have to land on the sea!" Lottie says.

"No!" replies the captain.

"But captain-"

"I said no! We can't. We just can't. If we land on the sea and not where we took off by the Lighthouse, we won't have flown around the world. We have to put the plane down on land!" the captain says. But he knows they probably will not make it all the way back to the Lighthouse. He knows it is safer to put the plane down gently on the sea and then swim the rest of the way or wave down a life boat. But the captain also knows how much this trip has meant to him. How important it is for him to finish it and to succeed the way he always hoped. The captain begins to cry. He takes off his goggles and wipes his eyes. Lottie notices but does not say anything. She knows why he is sad.

"Alright," says the captain. "Let's make an emergency landing at sea." He starts to push the steering wheel down and head towards the water. More and more tears fill his eyes and they sparkle in the sunset. His eyes start to look like rockpools, full of hope and disappointment. The captain had spent his whole life planning the trip. He had been working on the design for the airplane since he was a small boy. His father attempted the trip once but could not do it, so he asked the captain when he was a boy if he would try and do it in his memory. The captain agreed, of course. But now he will not be able to make his father proud. Just like him, he will not complete the trip. The captain wipes his eyes with his handkerchief.

I can't bear seeing him like this, Lottie thinks. This trip has always meant so much to him. He has taught me everything I know about flying. It is because of him that I am here flying in this spectacular airplane today. I cannot let these years go to waste, she thinks.

"No we are not!" she yells.

"Huh?" grunts the captain.

"We are not going to be making an emergency landing on the sea. We are going to land next to the Lighthouse, right where we took off!" says Lottie.

The captain looks up, his tears drying in the wind. "But we won't make it," he says.

"We've made it this far, haven't we? We just need to peddle like we've never peddled before," Lottie says.

"There's no use," says the captain. "We may as well land in the sea. Maybe the journey was never meant to be completed. Maybe I'm just not good enough."

"Yes you are! We are here because of you. We have almost travelled around the world in a peddle airplane because of you. And now we will land by the Lighthouse. Because... well, because I have not spent most of my young adult life peddling a wooden airplane just to not complete our journey! Now, are we landing by the Lighthouse or what?"

The captain lifts his head out of his hands and looks at Lottie with a smile that covers his whole face and stretches from his mouth to his eyes.

"Are we? Or what?" Lottie repeats.

"We're landing by the Lighthouse!"

"That's right!"

The captain grips the steering wheel and lifts up, pulling the airplane back higher in the sky. It is a difficult challenge to control the airplane now the left wing is almost entirely gone. But the captain has flown through storms and through the eyes of tornadoes, if any team can fly a plane with a missing wing, it is him and Lottie.

The team peddle harder and harder, trying to lift the plane high enough over the approaching cliffs. Below, Lottie watches seagulls dip and dive over beach-goers, fishing boats with no fish, and life boats zooming across the sea. Soon, the great shadow of the Lighthouse in front of the Sunday evening sun is much more than a distant image. Now, Lottie and the captain can see the windows, the doors, the birds sitting on the top, smoke rising from chimneys, and steam on the insides of windows. Their target is approaching. And fast.

The pair keep peddling as hard as they can. The plane is struggling higher into the sky, but it is not yet high enough to make it over the cliff edge.

"Peddle harder!" the captain shouts.

"I am!" Lottie shouts back.

The cliff is coming towards them like a bullet train. Before they know it…

CRASH.

THUD.

The captain and Lottie open their eyes. They are both pleased to know that they are alive. They look around them and see the grass on either side and the Lighthouse on their right. The plane just made it over the cliff, breaking off the wheels and sending the aircraft skidding across the grass. The plane slides past the Lighthouse and into the crowd who are applauding and cheering on the captain and Lottie.

"We did it!" the captain says. "Because of you, Lottie. Thank you."

Lottie smile and squeezes the captain's hand. "Sometimes," she starts. "If you have a dream that you know is possible. You should do everything you can to make it come alive. Believing in yourself, determination and teamwork is the recipe for success."

Then the pair climb out of the airplane and are carried on the shoulders of the crowd into the sunset.

8. RU AND GRANDMA HAVE SEEN THE WORLD

Ru and Grandma have been lying on their stomachs looking out at the sea and the world. Ru cannot believe what she has seen. All of the stories, all of the tales, all of the adventures and danger, friendship, love, teamwork, determination and courage. You really can see the whole world from up here, she thinks. If you have friends and relationships like the stories down there do, that is the world at your fingertips, or on the edge of your fin, or tucked within a shell. The world is made up by you and me, and everything in between. All the things that connect us and make us who we are… that is what the world is.

"How was that?" asks Grandma.

"Amazing," Ru replies.

"And not boring?" Grandma asks.

"Not even a little bit," Ru says.

"So, will you come up here again? Without me next time?" Grandma asks, helping Ru up to her feet.

"Yes! I love it up here," says Ru.

"And you see, Ru. If you had not have faced your fears of heights and your fear of the 100th floor, we would have never seen everything that we have seen. It is only because of your courage and bravery that we have had the day that we have had. We would have missed everything out there, if you had not taken the first step. It is all because of you."

"But you helped me, Grandma," says Ru. "You helped me up the steps and it was you who wanted me to come up here."

"Oh, Ru," says Grandma. "I did not make you do anything. You did it all. I just helped you make your decisions."

Ru smiles. She realises that she faced her fears and had the most amazing day because of it. She can barely believe the adventures that she has had. She takes Grandma's hand and opens the hatch. Benny jumps down onto the step and then takes each step at a time with Ru and Grandma, purring along the way. They all feel incredibly calm. They know how special the world outside the window is. They know all of the wonderful stories that are waiting for them. Ru knows that next Sunday another whole world of adventures will be waiting for her. And she cannot wait.

Ru and Grandma take their seats around their dinner table. Benny climbs onto his bed. The warmth of the kitchen and the smell of roast chicken sends him straight to sleep. Ru's Mum brings over the last of the food. The steamed beans. The roast potatoes. The cauliflower cheese. Volcanoes of steam erupt into the air.

"So," Ru's Mum starts. "Did you two have a good afternoon?"

Ru smiles at Grandma. Grandma smiles at Ru.

"The best," Ru says.

The End

DISCLAIMER

This book contains opinions and ideas of the author and is meant to teach the reader informative and helpful knowledge while due care should be taken by the user in the application of the information provided. The instructions and strategies are possibly not right for every reader and there is no guarantee that they work for everyone. Using this book and implementing the information/recipes therein contained is explicitly your own responsibility and risk. This work with all its contents, does not guarantee correctness, completion, quality or correctness of the provided information. Misinformation or misprints cannot be completely eliminated.

Printed in Great Britain
by Amazon